A SECOND SHOT AT LOVE

A TOWNSBURY PERFECT STORM NOVELETTE

KERRY EVELYN

A Second Shot at Love: A Townsbury Perfect Storm Novelette

Edited by Megan Fuentes and Chris Kridler

Cover design by Megan Fuentes

Interior formatting by Erika Everest at Eddally Publishing

This story first appeared in *Sweet Romance: An Anthology*, published by Craig Martelle, LLC.

Published by Swan Press

ISBN (ebook): 978-1-7361977-0-7

ISBN (print): 978-1-7361977-4-5

❀ Created with Vellum

To Craig, Las, Erika, and the #Sweeties

There is a time for everything,
and a season for every activity under the heavens:
a time to be born and a time to die,
a time to plant and a time to uproot,
a time to kill and a time to heal,
a time to tear down and a time to build,
a time to weep and a time to laugh,
a time to mourn and a time to dance,
a time to scatter stones and a time to gather them,
a time to embrace and a time to refrain from
embracing,
a time to search and a time to give up,
a time to keep and a time to throw away,
a time to tear and a time to mend,
a time to be silent and a time to speak,
a time to love and a time to hate,
a time for war and a time for peace.

— Ecclesiastes *3:1-8*

To Craig, Las, Erika, and the #Sweeties

There is a time for everything,
and a season for every activity under the heavens:
a time to be born and a time to die,
a time to plant and a time to uproot,
a time to kill and a time to heal,
a time to tear down and a time to build,
a time to weep and a time to laugh,
a time to mourn and a time to dance,
a time to scatter stones and a time to gather them,
a time to embrace and a time to refrain from embracing,
a time to search and a time to give up,
a time to keep and a time to throw away,
a time to tear and a time to mend,
a time to be silent and a time to speak,
a time to love and a time to hate,
a time for war and a time for peace.

— *Ecclesiastes 3:1-8*

1

A guttural cry from Gil Spurgeon, the Townsbury Perfect Storm's burly defenseman, shot straight to Sarah Hutchinson's soul. She halted midway through loosening his laces. "Easy, Gil. I have to get this skate off. Grab onto the bench for support."

He sucked air through his teeth as she made quick work of the laces, carefully maneuvering the boot from his foot. Sarah flung her auburn ponytail over her shoulder, keeping her expression neutral as she peeled off his sock and examined the ankle. He'd taken a ninety-eight-mile-per-hour slapshot at the top edge of his boot just before the buzzer blared. Off balance, he caught his skate blade in a rut. He fell into an opposing player, and his foot twisted out from under him as he went down. Hard.

"Just needs ice, right?" His question was hopeful, but the look in the eyes of the thirty-three-year-old alternate captain bore the truth—the prognosis wasn't good.

She gave a sympathetic half-smile. "Looks like you might be getting some extra quality time with your new baby. You really do believe in taking one for the team, don't you?"

"Just doing my job. It stayed out of our net, didn't it?" He flashed her a toothy grin.

"Oh, yeah. You're done for today, though." *And probably the rest of the season.*

"Yeah, I figured." Gil sat back and looked out over the crowd. "Hey, Sarah, not to freak you out, but there's some dude a few rows back staring at you. I thought he was staring at me at first, but he's definitely checking you out."

Sarah didn't have time or patience for hockey fans—or anyone—trying to get her attention. After her fiancé died two years ago, Gil and some other players had made it a point to look out for her. One of the many challenges that came with being a female trainer in a men's sport. Especially for a twenty-something former model.

She'd hated modeling, but it'd paid for school and led to the job she'd always wanted. For a while, all her plans had fallen into place.

Then Colin had been blown up in the Middle East. The only man she'd ever loved had been ripped away from her, along with the life they'd been building together.

Normally, she'd roll her eyes and ignore the attention. But this time, the hairs on the back of her neck prickled.

Sarah turned her gaze upward. "Holy hell." She locked on the intense, dusky blue eyes staring back at her from a face that haunted her recent dreams.

"I don't think I've ever heard you swear before. You know him?" Gil struggled to sit up. "Sarah? Hey, you okay? You look like you've seen a ghost."

"I—I—" Her ears rang, and her heart thumped painfully in her chest.

"Ow! Uh, Sarah—"

Giving a quick shake of her head, she loosened her grip on Gil's foot. "Oh, shoot, I'm sorry."

When she turned back, the man was gone.

~

Zach Miller spent the first two periods alternately watching the game and Sarah, waiting for a chance to talk to her. They'd only met briefly two weeks ago when his station lent support to a manhunt in an area where she'd rented a cabin. They'd shared a moment and a few quiet words of commiseration about the deaths of her fiancé and his brother.

After the FBI cleared her cabin, officers completed a final sweep of the area. Zach found something on the ground he was sure belonged to Sarah and had finally decided to ask a mutual friend for her phone number. Unfortunately, calling her had proven to be more difficult than he expected.

Upon learning her team would be in town to play the Acadia Harbormasters, he'd bought a ticket to the game, a few rows behind the opposing players' bench, and waited for the right time. When the horn sounded the end of the period, the home team's star defenseman hadn't gotten up. Two of his teammates helped him to the bench, where Sarah now tended to him.

When the stretcher rolled in, Zach's sense of urgency grew. He had to talk to her before she left. He shuffled past the spectators in his row, apologizing while keeping Sarah in sight.

She'd consumed his thoughts, and not just because of the charged circumstances of their meeting. No, it'd been much more than that. In the cabin, he'd looked into the blue depths of her sad eyes and recognized the pain hidden there—the same pain he saw every time he looked in the mirror. In that moment, after six years, a long-absent feeling of peace had washed over him.

Had she felt a similar wave of emotion?

Zach was halfway around the arena when Sarah looked up from the injured player and noticed him, her rosy cheeks paling. He'd known he might be an unwelcome reminder of her harrowing experience. The last thing he'd wanted was to cause her alarm, but it was important that he see her.

Never losing sight of her as they loaded the player onto the stretcher, he continued wading through the crowd grabbing concessions and milling about between periods. He yanked his ever-present pocket journal from his jacket, scribbled a note, and ripped the page free.

"Sarah!" The name flew from his lips with a hint of desperation, not how he'd imagined it. He cringed inwardly and squared his shoulders. Now was not the time for his insecurity to rear its ugly head. He was a cop, after all. Hesitation on the job could mean the difference between life and death.

Oddly, in this moment, that was exactly how he felt. *Assert your strength.* He used his command voice when he called her name a second time.

Sarah whirled around, her mouth dropping open. Uncertainty flickered in her eyes.

He leaned over the barrier and held the paper in his outstretched hand. "Take this, please."

Her eyes dropped to the note, then lifted to meet his. He held his breath until, finally, she inched closer, extending a shaking hand to snag the note before heading into the tunnel.

Zach watched her until she cast a questioning glance over her shoulder, then disappeared out of sight. He thought of the small but significant box back at the station and its precious contents, and hoped she'd call him before her team returned to Boston.

2

The next day, Sarah sat at her kitchen table, absently pushing the now room-temperature grilled chicken around her plate. The note she'd tossed into the catch-all basket with her keys and miscellaneous mail called to her. She'd awakened that morning certain she'd be in a better headspace to read it. Hours later, it was still in the basket.

To say she'd been surprised to see Zach would be a major understatement. Had he attended the game specifically to speak to her? If so, she wasn't sure how she felt about that. And why did it feel like opening his note would upend her life? It was just words on a piece of paper, from her best friend's husband's cousin's friend. Zach was no one to her, really. But it had been important enough that he'd sought her out at the game.

Unease coursed through her veins and her heart pumped hard as she pictured Zach's face. Classic chiseled cheekbones and jaw. Kind baby blues she could get lost in. There was a vulnerability to him that she didn't see in the hockey players she worked with that made her wish he *was* someone to her.

"You're being ridiculous." Sarah shoved back from the

table and stood. Not giving herself a chance to change her mind, she snatched the note up and unfolded it.

Her hand flew to her mouth. The message was short:

Sarah—Dog tags belonging to Colin Charlton were found outside the cabin you stayed in. They aren't related to our case. Are they yours? Please call me. —Zach

Tears pricked the back of her eyes as a heavy weight lifted off her shoulders. She'd thought Colin's tags were lost forever. Sarah unplugged her phone from her charger and dialed the number written below his name.

One ring. Two rings—

"Hello?"

"Zach?" Her voice was a ragged whisper.

"Hey, Sarah. I'm so glad you called. Are you still in Maine?"

He got right to the point. Good. Keeping this strictly business made this much easier for her.

"No, I'm not. I'm ... um ... sorry I didn't call you last night. I was busy with my player, Gil. He had to undergo surgery." Okay, so that was only half true. "How long do I have to pick them up?"

"As long as you need."

His soothing voice took her back to their conversation in the cabin. It helped still her nerves then, and it was helping to calm her now.

"Um." Her calendar was packed the next couple of weeks. "I can't get there until March. And I'd rather not have them mailed to me." She'd never survive losing them again.

"I can bring them to you." His velvety reply caused an involuntary shiver.

"I can't ask you to do that. You live far—"

"I offered, and I have this weekend off. I don't mind. Honest."

Sarah twisted and smoothed her ponytail with her free

hand as she considered his offer. Maybe she could squeeze in some time.

She wasn't sure she wanted to be alone with him, though. The feelings he evoked in her were alarming. Feelings she shouldn't be having for another man.

You only get one soul mate.

Right?

But the fact that he'd drive Colin's dog tags to her—five hours each way—touched her deeply. "I've got this thing on Saturday. The Spurgeons are hosting a Sip-and-See to introduce friends to their new baby. Could you meet me there at five o'clock?"

They could do a quick exchange and he could be on his way.

"Sure. Text me the details."

"Okay." She ended the call before he could make small talk. There was no denying part of her wanted to get to know him better. But she needed more time.

~

Zach rang the Spurgeons' bell Saturday afternoon, his conversation with Sarah replaying in his head for the millionth time. She'd seemed in a hurry to get off the phone, and he hadn't pushed, knowing she still struggled with the loss of her fiancé. He hoped the tags would bring her comfort.

The door swung open, revealing a pretty blonde. "Hi, can I help you?"

He cleared his throat. "I'm Zach Miller. Sarah asked me to meet her here?"

"Oh! Yes, hi! I'm Reese Spurgeon. Pleasure to meet you."

"You, too." He shook her hand. "Congratulations on your new baby."

"Thanks. Come inside. It's freezing out." She waved him in

and shut the door. "Sarah should be here any minute."

Inside, a handful of couples sat around a spacious living room. At the far end, a broad-shouldered, dark-haired man held court from a massive microfiber sofa-recliner, his cast-encased leg elevated. A small pink bundle sprawled across his chest.

"That's my husband, Gil, and our daughter, Stefani. She's two months old and already has her daddy wrapped around her tiny little finger."

"She's adorable."

"Mmhmm. Even when she's fussing at three a.m." Reese sighed, her smile warm with a mother's love. "Why don't you take my spot next to Gil while I grab you a drink?"

"Um ..." Zach cast a quick glance at the assembled group regarding him curiously.

She leaned close and lowered her voice. "Don't worry, they've all been warned not to grill you."

"It's ... Well, I'm not sure I can stay." Had Sarah intended for him to stick around the party? The last thing he wanted to do was put her on the spot.

"Don't be silly. Meet the baby, have dinner, and stay for the game."

He hesitated. "Okay, thanks."

"Great! Beer?" Reese took his coat.

"Sure." One drink, and if Sarah seemed uncomfortable with him being there, he'd leave.

Zach watched his hostess disappear down a hallway. He turned back toward Gil and the others.

Gil grinned. "You better sit down before my wife comes back."

Zach chuckled, and a small amount of tension left his shoulders as he settled himself on the other side of the armrest.

Gil flattened one big hand over the baby's back and twisted

slightly to shake Zach's. "Welcome to our home, Zach."

"Thanks for having me. How's the ankle? I heard you needed surgery."

"Yeah, I'm out for the rest of the season. But that has its perks. I scored precious time with my Stefi girl." He kissed the top of his daughter's head.

Gil introduced him to the other couples, and Zach relaxed a bit more. As Reese started back his way, the doorbell rang. She all but tossed him the beer and hurried to the door.

Zach stood as Sarah entered and removed her coat. She glanced his way and gave him a small wave, but he noticed her lips purse and her throat move up and down. Apparently, he wasn't the only one who was nervous.

"Hi, Zach." She blessed him with a shy smile, and that zingy feeling whooshed through him again. "Thanks for coming."

"My pleasure." She sat next to him and folded her hands in her lap. Her orange and vanilla-scented ponytail invaded his senses as the warmth from her body touched his.

Zach took a long pull from his beer, trying to cool down. *Say something, anything, you idiot.*

Gil's voice cut through the tension. "So, Sarah, how's the planning coming with the Valentine charity gala?"

"Great..." Sarah gave him an odd look as she dragged the word out like a question. "According to Lanie, everything is on track. The committee is set to raise more money this year for the kids." She smiled warmly. "The gala benefits underprivileged athletes in the community, granting money for camps, equipment, things like that."

"Sounds awesome." Zach sometimes volunteered at a youth center working with at-risk kids. He knew all too well how much financial help they needed.

"So, Sarah, you don't have a date yet, right?" Gil tipped his chin up toward Zach. "I bet Zach would love to take you."

3

Oh, no. No, he did not. Sarah felt Zach's eyes on her and forced herself not to look at him.

"Yeah, Sarah, you missed last year." Ashton Blanchard looked over at Zach and grinned. "Turned down everyone who asked."

Sarah narrowed her eyes at him. "I was busy."

"Washing your hair?" Team captain Patrik Liška teased, remnants of his Czech accent sneaking into his speech. "C'mon, Sarah. We've got room for two more at our table. If you take him, you won't have to keep saying no to Houlihan." He chuckled.

Sarah rolled her eyes and shook her head. Houlihan, the rookie center, had been trying to charm her all season.

How could she say she didn't want to go without being rude?

"When's the fundraiser?" Zach asked.

"Next Saturday." All the guys answered at once.

Her breath caught in her throat when Zach's warm hand curved over hers. "Sounds fun. I'd love to take you." His eyes held hers, as if forcing her to really *see* him.

She should say no. Right? Or was it time for her to take a leap of faith?

Unable to pull away from his gaze, she drew back her shoulders. "Okay."

Leap of faith, it is.

~

As the night wore on, Zach sensed the battle brewing within Sarah. He didn't want her to feel trapped into attending the gala.

He was having a great time getting to know the group. It was obvious they all cared about Sarah and wanted what was best for her, and he wanted to pass whatever test this was.

The hockey game ended with the Bruins suffering a grueling loss to the Buffalo Sabres.

Sarah leaned toward him. "I need to get going. Walk me to my car?"

"Of course." He stood and offered his hand. After a brief hesitation, she placed her hand in his and held tight. The buzz of conversation in the room faded as they stared at each other. Zach's mind drew a blank as her blue gaze held him captive.

Gil pushed himself off the couch, balancing precariously, and clapped Zach on the shoulder. "Hey, man, where're you crashing tonight?"

Zach dragged his eyes away from Sarah. "I was planning to drive back."

"To Maine? This late?" Reese joined them. "Please, stay in our guest room."

He shot a glance at Sarah. "That's very generous, but—"

"You should." She seemed surprised by her words. "It's late."

He nodded. "Okay. Thanks."

Reese handed them their coats, and they said goodbye. As Zach watched her hug her friends, he reflected on his own support group, or lack thereof. He had friends, sure, but he mostly lived the life of a loner. He'd always been happy hanging out with his brother and his brother's friends. They'd done most of the talking and planning, and Zach tagged along.

When Dylan died, everything changed.

Tonight, he was reminded of what he'd been missing—true friendship.

Out in the biting cold, Sarah's shoulders drew up to her ears, and she wrapped her arms around herself as they hustled toward the vehicles.

Zach opened the passenger door of his truck, snagged a small box from inside the console, and handed it to her.

Her fingers shook as she removed the top. Light flashed off the small metal rectangles. After a moment of simply looking at them, she lifted them from the box, clasped them in her fist and held them to her heart. Her eyes dropped shut, and a tear slid down her cheek.

"Thank you," she whispered.

Zach opened his arms and she stepped into his embrace. Her tremble rocked his soul and sent a spark through him at the same time. Clutching her tighter, he whispered into her hair. "It'll be okay." This evening confirmed Zach's attraction to Sarah, and if her pounding heart was any indication, she felt it too.

"How can you know that?" She raised her head, their faces inches apart. "Today was the best day I've had in two years and twenty-eight days."

4

Taz Houlihan flashed a flirty smile at Sarah from his prone position on the table. She had his leg extended against the front of her shoulder and slowly pressed forward, stretching it as she strategically worked on his hamstring muscles.

"Ow!" The usually-cocky rookie grin gave way to a grimace.

"Too far?" Sarah asked innocently. "Gosh, I'm so sorry. I thought you could handle it."

"Oh, I can handle it." He waggled his eyebrows.

Sarah laughed. The eighteen-year-old was as goofy and as full of himself as one might expect a teenage professional hockey player to be.

"Sarah!" Lanie Saunders called from across the large, airy training room. She skirted around the equipment, phone in hand, a glare on her face.

"Everything okay?" Sarah asked, concerned. Her best friend had had a rough year and was juggling a lot of glass balls.

"When are you done with him?" Lanie asked.

"Gee, Lanie, you make me sound disposable." Taz stuck his bottom lip out in a mock pout.

"Not now, *Travis*." He winced at Lanie's growl. Phone to her ear, she turned to Sarah. "I've got Meemaw on the phone. She wants the scoop."

"The scoop?" Uh-oh. Lanie's husband's grandmother was infamous up and down the east coast for her well-meaning meddling. "Gimme just a minute."

Sarah finished Taz's hamstring and tried to ignore Lanie's tapping foot. "Okay, Taz. Don't move. I'll be right back."

Sarah wiped the sweat from her brow and motioned for Lanie to follow her into her office. "What's up?"

"You're not only going to the gala, but you're bringing a plus-one? Zach isa friend of Matt's cousin. Why am I the last to know?"

She sighed. "I'm sorry, Lanie. I—don't know." Why *hadn't* she mentioned it?

Through the phone, the elderly woman's voice was chatting away.

"She wants to talk to you." Lanie tapped the screen to change to a video call.

"Sarah, dear! How wonderful you've started dating again." Daisy Mae Saunders in all her poofy white-haired glory smiled back at her. "I just wanted to tell you myself I'm so glad you're back in the game."

Sarah chewed her lip, unable to express the doubts about getting involved with Zach that had begun to creep into her battered heart. "Thank you, but I'm probably going to cancel." She darted a glance at Lanie.

"Oh, don't do that! It's time, dear. It's devastating to lose someone you love. But you're remiss if you're trying to live *without* Colin. The love you felt for each other will always be there. You should be trying to live *with* the love he left behind. He wouldn't want you to spend your life alone. Would he?"

Boom. Sarah fought back tears, swallowing past the painful lump in her throat.

"No, ma'am," she whispered. "I ... I have to go." Sarah ended the call and handed the phone back to Lanie.

Lanie tucked it in her pocket and gave her a sad smile. "It's okay to cry, you know. Tension release?"

Sarah pulled her chair out from behind her desk. Lanie positioned herself behind her and began to knead Sarah's shoulders.

"I'm fine," Sarah sighed. "I think. Anyway, I've done enough crying the last two years to last a lifetime."

~

I'm looking forward to Saturday.

Delete.

Hi, Sarah, how was your Monday?

Delete.

Five days to go!

Delete.

Without sending a single text, Zach stepped out of his police SUV and shoved his phone into one of the pockets in his tactical vest. Frozen grass crunched beneath his boots as he approached the familiar headstone. The biting chill of the starlit February night sliced straight to his bones.

Beneath him, six feet down, lay his brother Dylan, who'd died of exposure on a night very much like this one.

"Hey, Dyl." He crouched down and swept dried leaves from the headstone. "I met someone. But you probably already know that, huh?"

Zach pulled off his glove and traced the crossed hockey sticks that were carved into the cold granite. Dylan had been a star player in his teens, turning down an opportunity to play semi-pro when it would take him away from the town and the people he loved so much.

"You'd definitely like her. She's a Bruins fan."

He shoved his hand back into his glove and sat on the ground. Closing his eyes, he embraced the cold swirling around him.

What would today look like if Dylan hadn't died six years ago? His brother and Hollis would be married. Maybe even have a couple of kids who spent weekends with Uncle Zach at his cottage by the sea. Motoring around the harbor in the boat.

The fantastical thoughts whispered away, replaced by the loneliness he felt whenever he thought about his brother.

"I went to see Hollis last week. She still believes if she hadn't canceled on you, you wouldn't have picked up that extra shift. And if I'd listened to you and gone to the police academy after college instead of the military, I would've been here that night." His voice cracked. "Nothing, not even a blizzard, would've stopped me from finding you."

He could almost hear Dylan's voice in his head arguing with him.

"Sarah lost her fiancé a couple of years ago. We connected ... I really like her, and it kills me to think of her living with the same kind of pain Hollis has since you died. I think ... maybe we can help each other. I want to try, at least."

Zach stood and pulled his phone from the pocket, tugging off his glove again, this time to send a text message to Sarah.

Thinking about Saturday. It's been a long time since I've been on a date. We'll figure this out together?

5

Sarah didn't sleep well with thoughts of Zach invading her mind. Her eyes were gritty and burning when she arrived at work the next morning.

"You doin' all right today, Sar?" Ashton fell into step beside her in the hall. His thick Boston accent blanketed her with a welcome security.

"Yeah, Ash, thanks." She forced a smile. "Didn't sleep well, you know?"

Keeping busy, that was the key to surviving today.

"I do." He averted her eyes and adjusted the strap of his bag.

"Still pining for Zoe, I see." To see Ashton mope was unusual, especially over a woman. "No plans today?"

"Game night. Besides, we're going to the gala together."

"Whatever you say. But it's Valentine's Day, so if it's more than that—and I'm guessing it is by the way you were acting like a lovesick puppy last Saturday—you should call her. Today. Don't wait. You've got several hours between the morning skate and the game. Make it count."

He grunted. "I don't know."

"If I have to convince you, maybe she isn't as important to

you as you think." Sarah stopped outside the locker room. "But if she's your lobster, don't mess around."

"My lobster?"

Sarah shrugged. "They mate for life. Time is something you can never get back, Ash. Believe me, I know."

Sarah left him with that heavy thought and headed to her office. Why was it so easy to give advice, but so hard to take it?

All day she'd tried to focus on doing her job, forget the memories, and push aside the guilt she felt over liking Zach. She wanted to see if there was more between them than friendship, but the loss of Colin was still too raw. Everywhere she looked, she was flooded with reminders that today was Valentine's Day, from the team's pink and red jerseys to the sweetheart cam during time-outs.

The Storm had defeated the Albany Hilltoppers at home, but it'd been a physical victory—over a hundred checks. They'd be hurting tomorrow.

As would she, just not physically. But she planned to stay as busy as possible to keep her mind from the memories of the Valentine's Day three years ago, when Colin had proposed.

Later that night, it was all she could do to hold herself together long enough to make it home.

Sarah toed the boxes at her front door to the side as she keyed open the lock. Her guilt magnified, knowing they contained the dresses she'd ordered for the gala.

In her bedroom, she set the boxes side by side on the duvet, stepped back, and stared at them.

Her fingers itched to grab the biggest, boldest black marker she owned and scratch *Return to Sender* all over and leave them outside. But another part of her, the little girl within, wanted to tear open the boxes and play dress-up. Only she wasn't an innocent child—she was a pain-scarred almost-widow who knew emotional upheaval lurked within all that cardboard and tissue paper.

"All right, Gingerlocks, let's see which dress fits just right." Recalling the nickname given to her by player Dane Blanchard, a fellow redhead, lightened her spirit a little.

As she opened the first box, Sarah was bombarded with memories. The last time she'd been dress-shopping, it'd been for her wedding with her sisters and Lanie. She'd found *the* dress, and Colin had video-called from overseas.

That call ended after an explosion on the other side of the screen.

She blinked a few times, stiffened her spine, and slipped the first dress over her head. *Too sexy.*

The next box held a black, long-sleeved number. *Too somber.*

The third, a wispy ivory-blush chiffon, floated around her legs like a cloud, and the silver-ombré sequins shimmered across the fitted bodice. The woman staring back in the mirror looked renewed, beautiful, and *alive.* The easy confidence and proud posture of her modeling days returned in her reflection. *Just right.*

She pictured Zach on her arm and froze. Fresh tears stung and spilled down her cheeks as the clock struck midnight.

Valentine's Day was officially over.

How could she think about moving on when she still felt so much pain? Sarah recalled her conversation with Ashton. Recognizing the mutual exchanges between him and Zoe convinced her they were in love and didn't want to address it. *Lobsters.*

Sarah had thought for sure Colin had been her lobster.

For life.

She lifted the delicate chain hanging from her neck and studied the diamond solitaire on the gold band. A symbol of a promise she'd intended to keep forever.

Until death do us part. They'd never gotten the chance to say those words to each other.

Did forever end with Colin's death? She wasn't sure.

Sarah reached for her phone to text Zach. *I'm so sorry.... I just can't do it.*

~

ZACH WAS WATCHING sports commentary on his phone when Sarah's text came through. His heart sank like an anchor, a gradual drop until it came to rest with a thud on the ocean floor. Before he could think it through, he called her. After six rings, her voicemail picked up. He understood her grief, more than she probably knew. The understanding didn't negate his disappointment.

He texted her. *It's okay, Sarah. I understand.*

Right now, the important thing was that she knew he was willing to wait as long as it took for her to feel ready to move on.

Zach tossed and turned until he finally gave up on sleep just before six a.m. He showered, dressed in extra layers, and filled a thermos with coffee.

The sun's bright orange-gold rays were just beginning to paint the horizon as he shuffled down the path from his cottage to the private dock. He needed to clear his head, and the fifteen-degree morning weather seemed like a good way to start his day off.

At the end of the dock, Dylan's boat bobbed and gleamed as it caught a ray of morning light. Zach picked up his pace and stepped onto the wooden planks, careful not to slip on the thin layer of icy frost. The boards creaked in protest under his heavy boots. He carefully climbed aboard and took his place behind the wheel.

Zach set his coffee in the cupholder as he felt an urgency to *go*. A few seconds later, the boat rumbled to life, its sound shattering the morning's stillness.

Save for routine maintenance over the years, the boat was as Dylan had left it, from the ratty UMAINE hoodie stashed in the cabin to the framed picture of Hollis on the keychain, even the Zdeno Chara bobblehead on the dash. Zach tapped the plastic likeness of Dylan's favorite player with his finger and set it jiggling. The action elicited a sad smile, bringing back favorite memories of traveling down to Boston every winter to watch a Bruins game or two with their parents.

He'd connected with Sarah watching the game Saturday night. Working for the team's affiliate, she'd shared inside stories he knew his brother would've loved to hear.

When the engine warmed, Zach eased the craft into open water, slowly picking up speed as he exited the no-wake zone. With a flash of determination, he pressed the throttle forward and worked up to top speed.

This was where he felt most alive, out here in the harbor, slicing through the liquid blue, connected to his brother. The simple act of taking the boat out, even briefly, eased his heart and helped him get past the heaviness. Did Sarah have a ritual when her grief became too much to bear?

An hour later, he was walking up to his back door when his phone rang. Zach dug the phone from his pocket, thrilled to see Sarah's name on the screen.

He used his teeth to pull off his glove and answered. "Hey there, Sar—"

"I'm sorry. I mean ... about last night," she cut him off. "I—I wasn't in a good place."

"It's okay, really." Zach sat on the rocker on his back porch, not ready to leave the cool morning air. "I understand."

"You're not disappointed?" Was that a hint of regret in her voice?

"I am, but I get it."

Her voice softened. "Yeah, I guess you do, don't you?"

"I do."

She sighed. "Do I hear birds?"

"Yeah, I live on the harbor. Seagulls year 'round."

"Sounds nice." The sadness in her voice tugged at him. "You're out early."

"Yeah. It's peaceful." His mind jumped to thoughts of taking her out on the boat with him.

What would happen if he and Sarah started dating and became serious? Would she be willing to relocate? Would he? The thought of leaving the cottage—the home he'd shared with his brother—tore him up inside.

No, he could never give it up.

Where did that leave them?

6

In the dark living room, backlit by the kitchen light, Sarah snuggled little Stefi Spurgeon to her chest. Her eyes closed and she stroked the baby's downy-soft hair, inhaling the powdery scent.

Due to back-to-back home games, Gil and Reese were celebrating their Valentine's Day a day late. Sarah volunteered to babysit, thinking one chill baby would be a piece of cake compared with caring for her sister's twins.

She'd been wrong. Stefi made her think about what could have been.

For so long, her response was always "I can't." *Nothing can hurt you if you don't take a chance, right?* Somewhere, without realizing it, she'd given up on the "I cans."

Colin died, but that didn't mean her dreams of a family, of motherhood, died with him. She could still have all those things, but only if she allowed herself to.

Was it possible she was moving beyond the pain of Colin's death?

Zach's handsome face filtered through her mind. She wanted to call him and apologize again for canceling. Mostly, she wanted to hear his voice and tell him how much she liked him and couldn't stop thinking about him. Would he want to see her again?

Five ... four ... three ... two ... one. Sarah sucked in a deep breath and snatched up her phone, tapped the video call icon and waited. The countdown technique always pushed her when she was afraid.

"Hey, Sarah." Zach appeared on the screen, looking surprised to hear from her.

"Hey. I ... I just wanted to call to apologize again." Her voice wavered. "I really did want to see you this weekend. But ..."

"No need to explain or apologize." He ran his hand through his wavy golden hair. Butterflies pounded in her gut. His sincere expression was everything to her in that moment.

"I—don't think you quite do. I just now figured it out myself." He opened his mouth to speak, and she said, "Please hear me out?"

"Of course."

Sarah tightened her hold on the sleeping baby. "It's not that I'm not ready to date—I want to, truly...it's—I —I'm afraid, Zach."

There, she said it.

Deep breaths. Keep going.

"I'm afraid of how much I like you. I'm afraid of leaving Colin behind, and—" She choked back a sob. "But, I'm also afraid of what I'll miss if I *don't* leave him behind."

Her chin quivered, and she lowered her cheek to the baby's head, drawing comfort from the warm bundle in her arms.

Zach remained silent, letting her find her way.

She swallowed. "I don't want to grieve forever." Her last word was barely audible.

"I don't want you to grieve forever either, Sarah."

She lifted her gaze to the screen, surprised to see Zach's

eyes shimmering, and willed herself to continue. "But how? How do I move forward?"

"One minute, one hour, one day at a time." He appeared to gather himself. "Listen, if you're up for it, I'd still like to see you this weekend. Charity gala or not."

"I'd like that, too."

"Saturday morning?"

"Yes." The front door deadbolt clicked. "Sounds like Gil and Reese are back. Can we talk when I get home?"

"I'll be here."

"Okay."

He'd been there, and picked up on the first ring. They'd talked for hours, and for the first time in over two years, Sarah had no difficulty falling asleep.

ZACH'S HAND shook as he rang Sarah's doorbell Saturday morning.

She flung open the door and greeted him with a shy grin.

"Hey." He held out his arms, and she fell into them. Zach wrapped an arm around her back and used the other to cradle her head to his chest. "I'm so glad you invited me," he whispered. "Ready to go?"

"Yes," she mumbled into his chest.

Zach had no plans of breaking that hug. He was letting Sarah set the boundaries, and if she wanted to hug him for five minutes—or five hours—he'd go with it. Holding her, he felt joy he'd been missing for so long pulse through his veins.

She stepped back and he followed her inside the apartment. "Nice place."

"Thanks. It's small but cozy. I like it."

"My place is small and cozy, too. The limo should be here any minute."

"The limo? But we're not—"

"Gil rented it for the day. I'm staying with the Spurgeons and he wouldn't take no for an answer."

Sarah half-smiled. "Can't be mad at him for meddling. But I feel bad that you guys have gone to all this trouble and—"

"Sarah, relax. It's okay." He took her hand. "And since we have it for the day, I thought maybe you could give me a tour of your town? Show me your favorite places?"

She nodded slowly. "Okay. Yeah. Let's do it."

Twenty minutes later, the limo slowed to a stop in front of The Plex. The driver put the car in park.

Zach leaned forward and addressed him through the open partition. "Don't worry. I've got it."

He opened the door and offered his hand to Sarah. She bit her bottom lip and placed her mittened hand in his. Her light squeeze sent shocks up his arm and straight to his heart.

They scanned the collection of buildings. "This is my home away from home," she said fondly.

"It's impressive. Are they all connected?"

"Yep. Let's go." She tugged him toward the main entrance.

Sarah had a story for every room of the massive sports complex, from the training areas to the ice rink. As she spoke about the Plex, her voice held the same love and appreciation he felt for his cottage.

After the tour, they ate lunch in the café before returning to the limo. Over the next couple hours, they explored the downtown center, drove around her college campus, and cruised by her parents' and older sister's homes.

"One more stop," she said and leaned forward to give the driver directions. A few minutes later, they pulled up to the entrance of Kimford Farm.

He shot her a quizzical look. "A farm?"

"Not just any farm. This one has everything from bumper cars to a country store." She directed the driver down a lane off the main entrance. "The ice cream stand—and pretty much everything else—is closed for winter. The walk-up hot chocolate window is open inside the store, though."

The limo stopped in front of the store and, once again, Zach opened the door. The driver tipped the brim of his hat, pulled away and parked in the small lot to wait for them.

After buying hot chocolate, Sarah took his hand again. "I want to show you something." She led him down a path that led behind the store. "This is the Merrimack River."

An empty bench sat nearby, and she guided him to it. They sat in comfortable silence watching and listening to the water rush past, sipping the steamy beverages in the chilly air.

"The other night when I called you ... I was..." She hesitated. "I wanted to tell you..."

He wrapped his arm around her lightly, hoping the comforting gesture would help her get the words out.

"When I saw Colin at the funeral home ..." she stared across the river, lost in her memories. "It didn't even look like him."

Zach pulled her against him.

"I told myself it wasn't real, that it wasn't him. But I saw the strawberry birthmark where his hair parted and knew it was, and I felt the devastation all over again." She took a deep breath and swallowed. "Then I ... I took out the tiny folded scissors I carry in my purse and cut a lock of his hair." Her eyes scanned the riverbank, then the sky above. "This was Colin's favorite place, so I came here, bought a rose in the store, tucked the hair into the petals, and tossed it into the river."

Zach squeezed her shoulder, and she rested her head against him, the pom-pom on her hat tickling his chin.

"We still don't have any details about what happened to him. It's classified." Sarah's voice became stronger with each word spoken. "I think that makes it even harder. How am I supposed to get closure without an explanation?"

"Faith," Zach whispered. "It's all there is. Faith that his life wasn't for nothing. Faith that he loved you until his last breath."

She nodded. "He did love me. And that's why I think he would understand this. Us." She took a lengthy pause. "Do you think it's too late to go to the gala?"

7

Sarah put the finishing touches on her makeup and looked in the mirror. The image staring back at her looked effervescent and bright.

Earlier, she and Zach stopped by Colin's parent's house. She wanted them to have their son's dog tags and the engagement ring, which had belonged to Colin's grandmother. Returning the items felt right.

It was time for her next chapter.

She'd come home after that to get ready for the gala, and Zach went to Gil's. When the doorbell rang announcing his return, Sarah released a long breath before swinging it open. Zach, handsome and strong, stood on her stoop in a perfectly fitted tuxedo.

Her cheeks heated. "You look amazing."

"Thank you, but you're taking my breath away."

She knew the feeling.

Zach escorted her to the limo, where the rest of their party awaited. Sarah sat pressed to his side, her head on his shoulder. His body warmed her as her friends chatted around them.

"Right, Sarah?" Ashton asked.

She blinked. "Hm?"

Zoe giggled and leaned forward. "Ash told me you lit a fire under him on Wednesday to take me out. Thanks." She placed a hand on either side of Ashton's head and drew his face down. They met halfway in a steamy kiss.

Sarah smiled and cast a sideways glance at Zach. He brought her hand to his lips and kissed her knuckles. Her eyes fell to his mouth, wondering what it would feel like to kiss him.

One thing was for sure. She wanted to.

Tonight.

The limo pulled up to The Plex's conference center. Sarah held tight to Zach's arm as they followed the players down the red carpet. They maneuvered around the reporters and weaved their way through the partygoers to find the coat check.

Sarah scanned the room. Off to the side, Lanie pored over a tablet. She looked up and smiled as Sarah approached with Zach. "You're here!" She rushed over to wrap Sarah in a tight hug.

"Zach, this is my best friend, Lanie, and her husband, Matt."

"It's so wonderful to finally meet you." Lanie hugged Zach. "I'm glad you came."

"Nice to meet you, Zach." Matt offered his hand, and they exchanged small talk about work and their military experiences.

"Okay, you two, enough chitchat. Go have fun!" Lanie commanded.

"We'll see you out there." Sarah took Zach's arm and led him deeper into the room, where conversations and music mingled. She spied the parquet dance floor as they found their table. "Do you dance?"

"I do." One dark brow arched up. His low baritone washed

over her like a gentle wave, stilling her nerves and radiating that peace she'd come to rely on in his presence.

She set her purse on the table. Sarah couldn't remember the last time she'd danced, and she didn't want to waste one moment of this night. "Let's not wait 'til after dinner."

Zach returned a smoldering gaze that caused her to shiver. As tall and built as any of her players, he cut an impressive figure. He took her hand and led her to the center of the dance floor.

Sarah's pulse kicked up as she relaxed into his embrace. They were the only ones on the floor, and she didn't care. Swaying in his strong arms, the outside world faded away. To be held by someone again ... No, to be held by *Zach* made her feel safe, cherished.

Who cared if they were the only couple dancing? It felt good to be in the moment. To be held in the arms of someone who made it clear that she mattered. That her future mattered.

One that he wanted to be a part of.

"Kiss him." Sarah jumped when Zoe whispered near her ear. Ashton gave a thumbs-up as they whirled away.

I think I will.

Sarah curled her arms around Zach's neck and smiled shyly at him. In his arms, she felt peace, security, and the familiar fluttering of rare connection. She brushed her fingers over his temple and let her fingers run through his hair, pulling his head down to hers. Realizing her intent, his eyes sparked and his embrace tightened.

When their lips touched, stars burst in a flash of blinding light behind Sarah's eyes, and the walls around her heart crumbled. Misery and grief faded away into the ether, and she knew that with Zach by her side, as he promised, everything would, in fact, be okay.

EPILOGUE

SIX WEEKS LATER

Zach slammed his tailgate closed and glanced back at the cottage. *You're not letting go. You're grabbing hold of something new and moving forward.*

Matt had approached him regarding a job with his company, providing disaster relief services. Zach had been ready for a change, and the move put him closer to Sarah. He'd fallen hard and fast for her over the last two months.

Her boots crunched behind him in the snow, and she wrapped her arms around his waist. "We'll be back soon, and your friends promised to look in on it while you're away." She swept snow from his shoulder. "Try not to worry."

"You're right." He twisted to kiss the top of her head. "I can't wait for you to see this place in the summertime."

"Every time I'm with you it feels like summer. I'm not cold anymore, Zach. And you're the reason why." Her eyes shimmered, no longer darkened by sadness.

Zach's heart melted at the impact of her words. "You're my sunshine, Sarah. No, not just sunshine. You're the flowers and the leaves underfoot and all the things that make life's seasons easier to bear." Zach tightened his hold and spun her around. Sarah's laughter floated in the air, music to his ears.

He slowed to a stop and set her down. His hands cradled her face. "Sarah, I—I know it's fast, but ... is it too soon to tell you I'm in love with you?"

She placed her hands over his and smiled. "It's not too fast. I love you, too, Zach."

He pressed his lips to hers, and their kiss held the promise of a spring filled with love and new beginnings.

AUTHOR NOTES

I hope you enjoyed Sarah's story! Her happy ending has been a long time coming!

Sarah and Zack first met in my short story, *A Night in the Cabin,* available on Amazon.

If you like sweet small-town love stories with a bit of suspense, turn the page to read the first chapter of Lanie and Matt's story, *Love on the Edge.* It's got everything romance readers love: an idyllic coastal resort, a fake marriage, a kickass heroine, a swoon-worthy bodyguard who loves his Meemaw, and a colorful ensemble cast of characters you won't forget!

For behind-the-scenes amazingness, the latest news, sales, and more, sign up for my newsletter at KerryEvelyn.com.

For the VIP experience, join my Facebook Reader group at Facebook.com/groups/CranesCoveCrew.

LOVE ON THE EDGE

Savannah, Georgia
5:22 a.m.

Matt Saunders bolted upright. A thick sheen of sweat covered his body. He gulped for air. He couldn't breathe. He couldn't think.

Flinging the covers, he dropped to the floor. Push-up after push-up wasn't enough to regulate his heartbeat. His biceps burned and his heart thundered as if it would leap straight through his chest. He rolled onto his back. Inhale, exhale. He crossed his arms against his chest. Up and down, up and down, up and down. He couldn't rid his mind of the pictures replaying over and over from the day his whole world changed.

Letting out a frustrated growl, he grabbed a discarded T-shirt out of his hamper and pulled on jogging pants. He couldn't get out fast enough. The apartment door slammed behind him as he took the stairs down two at a time.

He hit the pavement hard, pushing forward at top speed, wanting to run out of his own body. Conscious of every moving thing in his sight, his adrenaline became jet fuel, propelling him down East President Avenue. He continued over the Islands Expressway and turned off the road at the park. Finally able to stop, he bent in half, hands on his thighs, and exhaled slowly. He shook violently as he fought the body-racking sobs that threatened to overcome him. He raised his arms over his head and then across his torso, elbows bent, stretching his triceps. Still, he couldn't calm his body or his thoughts.

Whatever had awakened him had triggered the instincts he'd trained for in combat. Pushing his body physically was the only way to fight the images that threatened his peace.

Up in the trees, a Carolina wren announced the new day with a pleasant song. Matt glanced up and wished he could appreciate the songbird's innocence. Instead, he turned around and sprinted full speed out of the park for the two-mile run home.

An hour later, he could breathe again. Matt lay on his bed, staring at the ceiling, willing the terrible images out of his head.

~

Thursday, April 27, 2017. Slept with windows open. Big mistake. Woke to the smell of smoke. It brought it all back. Went for a run. Breathing again.

HE'D BEEN TOLD it would get easier. The more he wrote it down in his journal, the less painful it would be. The problem was that the pain kept the memories of his friends alive, which he hadn't been able to do on his own. The new medication allowed him to sleep most nights, but it didn't stop the triggers.

Matt dropped his pen as the vibrating phone interrupted

his journaling. His hand trembled as the name on the screen forced his heart to quicken again.

"Hello?"

"Saunders." Bright flashes returned as Colonel Owens's voice summoned him over the line. The smell of burning human flesh, the dark red blood of his comrades, the sound of the boom that had ripped up his leg.

"Sir?" Matt began to pace. His left hand squeezed his side, reminding him to stay upright and alert. The knuckles on his right hand turned white as he gripped the phone in earnest.

"I'm no longer your official superior." The colonel paused. "Saunders, I have a job for you. My granddaughter was attacked last week. Subject is on the run. She's recovering here for now. I want her to disappear for a while until we get this guy. How soon can you leave?"

Matt swallowed. He was no good to his brothers in arms overseas. He was possibly facing a medical retirement, which meant he may never again serve in an official capacity. This was his chance to do something, here and now. He was a protector, a soldier. Was it possible to keep his emotions and impulsivity under control well enough to keep the colonel's granddaughter secure?

"Sir, no disrespect, but are you sure I'm the guy for this job?" Matt could barely take care of himself some days. It had been several months since the blast, but he was still in therapy, with no end in sight. His leg had healed almost completely, thanks to his dedication to the physical therapy and his willingness to push through the pain. His mental health was another story. He'd be fine for days at a time, even weeks occasionally, and then something would trigger a flare, like this morning, and he was right back in the hellhole that had destroyed his life's purpose. Despair draped over him like a heavy cloak, engulfing him under its weight.

"You're exactly the guy for this job. You are the toughest, most loyal, most thorough soldier available. I'm proud of you, son, and the way you're working through your trauma. Your specific therapy was mandated for a reason, and I hear you're doing exceptionally well. You're on your way back, if that's where you want to go. And if they retire you, contractors are constantly hiring guys like you to ensure the safety of our troops and supplies. You can do this. You'll give it everything you've got. I wouldn't expect any less, and I wouldn't have called if I wasn't confident. I wouldn't trust my family to anyone but the best. I want you. Lanie's recovering and she's traumatized. Maybe you can help her with that."

"Yes, sir." Matt swallowed deeply, forcing down the lump in his throat. He closed his eyes, willing his breaths to come slowly and evenly. "I can leave Saturday."

"Good. I'll be in touch with further instructions."

Lanie Owens slumped against the plush pillows on the divan as her grandmother busied herself packing up the designer suitcase. Her eyes glazed over as the older woman chatted about the plan to go into hiding at a resort in Maine.

She closed her eyes. It had been over a week since she'd been attacked by her coworker. She'd always been polite and pleasant to him, but after she turned him down for a date, he began popping up everywhere. Her sister, Caroline, had warned her repeatedly not to be so friendly to him. I've got a bad feeling, Lanie, she'd told her. Caroline was always so dramatic, and Lanie had a heart for outsiders. She'd thought he just needed a friend. But a few weeks ago, she found him waiting outside her apartment door when she got home from work. When he got angry and refused to leave, she banged on her neighbor's door across the hall and called the police. A restraining order was set up, she filed a formal complaint at work, and he was let go.

But it wasn't enough.

He'd broken in during the night, determined to convince her they were meant to be together. She shuddered. Through the grace of God, she'd been able to fight him off, but not before he slashed at her neck and torso. The cuts were deep enough to require stitches, and she lost consciousness on the way to the hospital. Fear paralyzed her as she woke up to the beeping machines and a man's hand on her arm. It had been her grandfather's hand, but the panic resulting from his touch was enough for her to scream like she was being attacked all over again. *I'm going to get my best guy to protect you*, her grandfather had promised.

"Allaina," Gran said firmly. Lanie snapped out of her reverie. "Are you even listening, dear?"

"Hmm?" She blinked and focused on her grandmother's distraught expression. "I'm sorry," she mumbled. Tears welled in her eyes. She turned her head to the window, not wanting her grandmother to see the pain in her eyes.

Her grandmother placed the item she'd just folded into the suitcase and joined Lanie on the divan. She pulled her in close. "I know right now you feel your life may never return to normal. But it will. And we will do everything we can to make sure you're never hurt again." She pulled away and held Lanie's chin in her hand. "Understand?"

Lanie nodded.

"Then let's finish this up and get you to bed. Your Aunt Liza will be here at seven in the morning to remove those stitches before she goes into work at the pediatrician's office. Your grandfather wants to be off bright and early to beat the traffic."

"I still don't understand why it's necessary to go so far. Why can't I stay here?"

Gran sighed. "We've been over this. The resort is far away and secluded. It makes sense to hide you away where you'll be inaccessible, and after all you have been through, no one will be surprised that you wanted to go away to recover. You've never put anything less than one hundred percent into anything you've done. Why would your recovery be any different?"

"I guess it makes sense. But I still don't want to go."

Lanie stood up and went into the bathroom to gather her personal items. She shouldn't be going away. She should be at the sportsplex, giving physical therapy to her patients, working on implementing the new programs and charity events she'd created, coaching and teaching her tween swimmers for their big meet on Saturday, and providing relief to her massage clients. She was letting everyone down.

MATT TAPPED IMPATIENTLY on the steering wheel as he sat in the infamous Boston traffic on the Tobin Bridge late Sunday afternoon. He tried to will the cars ahead of him to move. Below him, the Mystic River twinkled in the sunlight. The crisp spring coastal air mingled with the exhaust fumes of seven lanes of traffic.

He'd declined the two-hour plane ride in favor of driving up the coast at his own leisure. The last time he'd been on a plane had tested every ounce of his self-control. The claustrophobic conditions he had felt onboard the aircraft months ago now resurfaced and pushed his every limit as he sat in the traffic.

He'd made good time on Saturday, getting through New York City before calling it a day. He'd planned to do some sightseeing in Boston before he headed up to Portland, where he would spend the night. He figured he could just drive around and stop wherever interested him, as tourists often did in Savannah. He had not been prepared for the congestion, lack of parking, and one-way streets of the bustling city. Hours passed and he hadn't seen anything except traffic, tunnels, and bridges.

A chill traveled down his spine and beads of sweat formed at his hairline. His palms felt clammy as he gripped the wheel, his knuckles white as he held on. He was grateful for the cool breeze passing through the open windows. You are not trapped. Feel your right foot on the brake pedal. Your other foot is resting on the floor. Your hands are on the steering wheel at ten and two. You are safe. You are not in a war zone. You do not need an escape route. Your heart is beating at a normal rhythm. Your lungs are taking in oxygen and expelling carbon dioxide. You are very much alive.

Matt's heartbeat began to slow. His palms loosened their death grip on the wheel. An involuntary shudder shook him as he forced his mind to overrule his body. Score another point for the therapist. As much as he's he'd resisted the therapy at first, he had to admit the tools he'd learned were useful. Self-talking made him feel ridiculous, but there was no doubt it was effective.

The traffic began to move as the wreck that had caused the backup was loaded onto a tow truck. He averted his eyes from the flashing lights of the rescue vehicles and willed his heartbeat to slow even further. Edging carefully past construction, he exited and merged onto I-95 North.

Finally free of the traffic, Matt felt the familiar rush of adrenaline. He pressed the gas pedal to the floor and shot out onto the highway, expertly navigating around an ancient Chrysler and a camper to get into the left lane. The road was clear as far as he could see.

You're out. Slow it down. Matt eased off the gas and held it steady at 70 miles per hour. He could barely rein in his own anxiety; how was he going to help the colonel's granddaughter with hers? The drive up the coast had drained him. He'd been lucky for the long stretches of light traffic, but it hadn't been enough to push away the claustrophobia or the memory of a similar road trip years ago with his best friend, whom he failed to save.

~

LANIE STARED through the passenger-side window at the Atlantic Ocean. Maine's rocky cliffs looked appealing. She wondered how many people had stood atop the rocks and contemplated life. Stop it, Lanie. You're being dramatic, like Caroline. Get a grip. Heaving a deep sigh, she tried once again to listen to her grandfather describe the man who was to be her bodyguard and the complicated security measures that would be put in place to ensure her safety. She shifted uncomfortably under the seatbelt. The skin at her neck where her aunt had removed the stitches earlier that morning felt raw and itchy.

"Matt's one of the toughest guys I've ever known. He went back in for the last man after the building was determined structurally unsound. They were both blown out of the building during a suicide bomber blast—the other guy didn't make it. Matt took a lot of shrapnel to his right leg, so you might notice he favors it when it's sore. But that doesn't make him unfit in any way," her grandfather assured her, glancing over uncertainly.

His fingers tightened on the steering wheel and he focused his eyes on the road ahead. His frustration was palpable in the confines of the car.

Lanie felt she should say something. "Sounds great, Grandpa." She shifted her gaze back to the window. "Thank you for setting this up until they find"— her voice broke —"that—"

"Someone had to," he mumbled.

Lanie hung her head. Once again, her grandfather had stepped in when her father had come up short in the fathering department. The colonel's son was everything he was not—entitled, indulgent, and completely unaware of everything outside his current periphery.

The police had been at a loss for where to even look for her attacker. Both she and her grandfather knew that her father was not about to spend extra money or time when he paid taxes for the police to do their job. Her dad had protested the Gulf War even while his own father was there risking his life. Her father had little use for authority, yet depended on the government to fix everything.

Lanie's grandfather had zero patience for his son. Because of his own experience with the evilest people on the planet, he consistently reminded her that she had to protect herself. In a life-and-death situation, you didn't have time to wait for help. You had to react and defend. It was the defensive techniques he'd taught her that had likely saved her life. If war was necessary, it was justified. He was as physically fit and sharp as a man less than half his age. He'd stayed in the army almost a decade past the usual retirement age on a special waiver, highly unusual and rare, but possible because of his effectiveness and likeability. Though he'd recently traded in his uniform for khakis and polo shirts, he was still 100-percent soldier and saw himself as his family's protector.

Colonel Owens could be tough, but Lanie knew he was warm on the inside. He still wore a fresh crew cut, despite only having a dusting of soft white fuzz remaining on his head. She wanted to reach over and give it a playful rub, as he'd ruffled the heads of all the grandkids when they were little.

Instead, she kept her hands in her lap, knowing he

wouldn't appreciate the distraction while he was driving. When Grandpa was serious, he was serious. And right now, he was serious about taking care of her.

Lanie thought about all he had done to ease her fear since the attack. In the last ten days, the colonel had reviewed the basic defense moves he'd taught her as a teenager, including how to break zip ties and fire a handgun. He'd given her a Life Alert necklace to wear around her neck in case of an imminent threat. She'd also been staying with him and Gran in their secure home, which was a mini-fortress compared to the weak security system her apartment building used.

The colonel turned right off Route 1 onto 186 and drove south toward Gouldsboro. Driving through Summer Harbor, Lanie could see the larger city of Bar Harbor across Frenchman's Bay. They drove in silence for some time. She stared out at the sea down below the cliffs. Whitecaps crashed with fury against the rocks. In other spots, waves caressed the pebbled beach before they pulled back out to sea. Based on the watermarks and seaweed on the rocks, high tide was approaching.

The harbor road wound through the pines, and Lanie lost herself in the tranquil scenery. Driveways framed by tall conifers led to homes deeper in the woods. She looked forward to the seclusion this façade of a vacation would offer.

Route 186 ended at Main Street and the little town of Winter Harbor displayed its charm. Her grandfather turned onto Beach Street and merged onto Crane's Cove Road. Up ahead, a small commercial center came into view.

Lanie sat up and took notice, mentally cataloging her surroundings as she had practiced with her grandfather. They passed a small park with a duck pond and playground, and a gas station with a mini-mart. Across the street was a fire station, a diner, and a small strip mall with a hair salon, boating supply store, and daycare. Diagonal from the diner, a three-story brick building housed a town hall, post office, and a state police station. A single state-trooper vehicle was parked on the side of the building. Ahead, a rotary displayed a large distressed wooden sign featuring a harbor seal bearing the greeting "Crane's Cove Welcomes You."

The colonel pulled into the Cliffside Diner and turned to his granddaughter. Lanie appraised the old train car that had been refurbished and remodeled into a restaurant. An addition had been built onto the back, and its sloped roof jutted proudly to the sky, prepared to expel the snow that would come in the colder months. The quaint structure endeared itself to Lanie because of her fondness for 1950s pop culture. Refusing to be afraid in this homey setting, she took a deep breath and reached for the door handle.

"I realize meeting Matt in person in a public setting for the first time isn't the best-case scenario, but this is a safe place. I know the owner; you can trust her. You've video chatted with Matt, so you're not seeing him for the first time. Don't let your nerves overpower you. You ready?"

"I've got to be," Lanie said. She opened the door and carefully stepped out, conscious of the slight pulling and tugging of tight skin where she'd been wounded. She put on her sunglasses to hide what was left of the faint bruises on her face. They were light yellow now and thankfully almost gone. Another day, perhaps two, her aunt had said. She shifted uneasily, turning her body slowly to ease the discomfort. Grabbing her purse with one hand and pulling on the support handle with the other, she stood up, closed the door, and looked around.

The colonel had taught her to be observant. She scanned the parking lot, where only a black SUV was parked. Across the street, two women watched four toddlers at the playground. No one else was around. At two, it was too late for lunch and too early to pick up kids from school. Lanie flipped her hood up over her new blonde curls and adjusted the dark sunglasses. Head down, she walked quickly into the diner as her grandfather held the door.

~

In the back-corner booth, Matt pretended to stare at the menu as he watched the tall, athletic blonde enter with the colonel. Behind the overlarge sunglasses that framed her oval face, he noted Lanie's medium-length curly blonde hair that cascaded out the front of her navy windbreaker. She'd had long chestnut waves when they video chatted.

He motioned over to Sadie, the waitress. She caught his signal, sauntered over to the table, and dropped off two more menus as they made their way toward him. She glanced at the colonel and raised an eyebrow. The colonel nodded at Sadie and she went back into the kitchen.

As they had planned, Matt stood up and allowed Lanie to sit on the inside of his side of the booth. The colonel slid in across from them. Matt put his arm around Lanie to give the appearance that they were together. She jerked away at his touch and glared at him. Concerned, he moved his arm to rest on the back of the booth. She shuddered, pressed her eyes closed, and inhaled deeply.

"I like your hair," he said.

"Thanks," she mumbled, her lips tight.

She slid her hood off and removed her glasses, revealing her fading bruises. Anger boiled deep in his belly, but he kept it in check. She was beautiful. What kind of deranged man would want to mar her perfect face? Her eyes, framed by long lashes and perfectly sculpted eyebrows, were as blue as the Atlantic at the base of the cliff. Her dainty nose was sprinkled with a dusting of light freckles, barely visible through the heavy makeup that coated her face. Her lips, pressed tightly together, shone with pink lip gloss. He studied her as she stared straight ahead at her grandfather intently, avoiding his gaze.

The colonel didn't waste any time with pleasantries. "Let's get right to the point, in case this restaurant is blessed with more patrons before we get a chance to talk." The colonel sat up tall as he nodded behind him to the empty booths. "I've reserved a cabin for you at the Cliff Walk Resort for the next month. Hopefully, we won't need all that time to find this scum. Sadie here is retired FBI and owns this diner. You can trust her if you need anything. I've hired a private detail out of a firm in Boston. His name's Jack Dalton and he's the new overnight security guard at the resort. Sadie knows the owners and set it up. They were told he is affiliated with the FBI and working undercover because of a homeland-security threat in the area. Since you live in a border town and that scumbag followed you across state lines and threatened you in New Hampshire, the FBI can work this case. Unfortunately, they won't expel the resources to get an actual agent up here, so we are doing this on our own."

Matt said, "We've been in contact. Jack checked in yesterday and has a room at the main lodge."

The colonel nodded and looked sternly across the table at Lanie. "You have any trouble; you press that button on the necklace I gave you. Matt will protect you if there is an imminent threat, and he'll set up a security system at the cabin to monitor activity around it at all times. You are never, under any circumstance, to leave his presence."

"Yes, sir." Lanie took a small bottle of lemon essential oil out of her purse, poured a few drops in her water glass, and took a sip. "If we're supposed to be married, don't we need rings?"

Matt took a small ring box out of his pocket. He opened it to reveal two silver bands, one inlaid with clear stones, the other plain. "It's not much, just cubic Z and sterling silver. I hope you like it." He flashed a grin.

Lanie cleared her throat. "It's great, really." She slid it on and wiggled her finger. "A little loose, but it probably won't fall off."

The colonel took an old-fashioned flip phone out of his jacket pocket and placed it in front of Lanie. "It's time to trade cell phones. This phone is untraceable." He looked at Matt. "We made it look as if Lanie left her apartment in a hurry to seek refuge. We planted a rumor that she's left the state, headed to visit her dad in New Hampshire. Hopefully, that will throw that piece of garbage off the track for enough time so that we can get him, maybe even draw him out. I'll retain her cell phone in case he tries to contact her. Any questions?"

Lanie stared down in disdain at the flip phone he'd placed in front of her. "Why the flip phone?"

"You'd be amazed what hackers can trace these days. And I don't want you tempted to log into email or social media. We're going to have your sister post that you're going tech-free while you recover."

Lanie frowned.

Matt felt an urge to make her want to smile. He called up the southern charm he had prior to his military experiences. "I promise to keep you safe, darlin', as long as you trust me," he drawled. He winked at her and smiled as her cheeks reddened. Reluctantly, he tore his gaze from her distressed expression. "Colonel, you can count on me. Thanks for trusting me."

"I know I can. It's a damn shame about that leg. There's not a lot of guys like you left out there."

Matt let out a long, slow breath and looked out the window past Lanie. "Don't I know it . . ."

The colonel nodded at Matt. "Won't be too much longer until you can be evaluated again. There's plenty of work if you know where to look." He shifted his eyes to Lanie. "We're gonna get this SOB. Make no mistake. No one hurts my granddaughter and gets away with it."

Lanie gave a weak smile. "Thanks, Grandpa." She shifted her body to face Matt. "Thank you for doing this. It couldn't have been easy to just up and leave your life for who knows how long. I want you to know how much I appreciate it."

A dark shadow passed over his eyes. "I'd do anything this man asked me to do. Besides, I don't have anything going on right now. And I may never get back out there at this rate. But hey, I'll do whatever God calls me to do. If I'm of better use to Him here lookin' after your pretty self, then I'm all for it." He smiled again, flashing his teeth this time. Matt wondered if he might be laying it on too thick. He hoped Lanie couldn't tell he was acting. He didn't want to sound condescending or arrogant.

The colonel nodded. "Then it's settled. Let's eat." He nodded to Sadie and she came over to take their orders.

The food arrived soon after, and Matt watched Lanie pick at her grilled chicken salad as he and the colonel reminisced about their time together in the Middle East.

"That last tour was pretty tough." The colonel shifted his eyes toward Lanie. "A lot of units came together to support the mission after the blast took out some of your guys."

Matt grimaced. He didn't have much of a unit anymore. Just a couple of wounded warriors who were trying to heal well enough to get back out there. The rest had returned to civilian life. "I heard."

"We lost some fine soldiers on that mission." The colonel looked at Lanie. "That was a tough one."

"Aren't all tours tough? You risk your life every time you go out there, Grandpa. You risk leaving family and friends behind. You risk your future and the future of those who are depending on you to come back," she said, a hint of pain in her voice.

It sounded to Matt like she knew this pain personally. "Did you lose someone out there?"

She nodded.

"It's always tough to lose a friend. I lost my best buddy out there."

Lanie breathed in slowly and closed her eyes. "I'm sorry. I know what you do is important, and necessary, and I'm grateful, I truly am. But please, let's talk about something else." Her tone closed the door to further discussion on the matter. Matt and the colonel exchanged a glance. The older man shrugged.

"So how are you liking retirement?" Matt asked the colonel.

"It's different. Finding that I have to learn how to relax. I believe I'm driving the missus a little crazy trying to keep myself busy." He grinned at Matt. "I've been gone as much as I've been home the last few decades, probably more if I were to keep track. I imagine I'm interrupting her groove."

Matt and Lanie laughed and the bell above the diner door rang. He noticed that Lanie hurried to pull on her large sunglasses to cover her eyes. Matt decided to change the subject again as two older couples settled into the booth two down from theirs.

"Well, I'm sure looking forward to getting started on this honeymoon! What time is check-in again, darlin'?" He grinned at Lanie and squeezed her closer to him. "Just play along," he whispered.

"Any time after three, sweetie."

Two booths down, a woman about the colonel's age craned her neck and smiled. "Couldn't help but overhear! Are you going to the Cliff Walk Resort?"

"Marge, mind your own business," the man beside her

grumbled. "Sorry, my wife here likes to make friends everywhere she goes."

"Oh, Harry, shush! If I didn't, we'd never have met Walter and Lil here." She gestured to the other couple.

"Humph," Harry said. He covered his face with the menu.

"We are," Matt replied, amused. "Are y'all staying there, too? We'd love some tips."

Marge beamed and made her way to their booth, her husband and friends looking on. She raised a brow at the colonel, who promptly slid over.

"Are you southerners? We live in the South now! Where are you from?"

Matt opened his mouth to respond, but she continued without pause.

"We love the Cliff Walk. This is our fifth year returning. Our first visit was our fortieth-wedding-anniversary trip, and we were blessed to meet Walter and Lil. We've been coming back every year since. There's so much to do, or nothing at all. It's so peaceful and nice to be away from the Florida heat. We're originally from southern New England but retired to Florida several years ago. We've made it a tradition of sorts to spend a few weeks here before we settle in with the family on Cape Cod for the rest of the summer." She leaned in conspiratorially. "We're snowbirds." She winked across the booths at her husband, who watched her with mild amusement. He had his arms crossed over his chest and one side of his mouth threatened to betray a smile. He never took his eyes off her.

"Walter and Lil are from Missouri. They say, 'Mizoura.' It's a hoot! Where did you say you were from?" This time she paused long enough to let Matt answer.

"Georgia. We—"

"Oh, we love Savannah. And Atlanta. And Helen. Such a fun state. What brings you here?"

"It's our honeymoon. We—"

Marge squealed. "Oh my, then I'll leave you be when I see you about. Harry, they're honeymooners! And who's this fine gent?" She nodded at the colonel.

"Colonel Gerald Owens, just passing through." He stuck out his hand.

Marge shook it graciously. "Very pleased to meet you. Harry! See? They're friendly, just as I said. They invited this gent to join them for lunch. He's just passing through."

Behind the counter, Matt noticed Sadie trying to hide her laughter. She must know this group well. Their eyes met. Sadie coughed and hurried back into the kitchen.

Matt smiled at Marge and offered his hand. "Very pleased to meet you. Matt Saunders. My wife here is Lanie. We were just finishing up so we can check in. Long drive up and such . . . looking forward to relaxin' with the missus," he added meaningfully, looking Marge in the eye.

"Of course you are, sweetie. Well, it was great to meet you. I'm sure we'll be seeing you around! And next time I want to see pictures of your big day. I bet they are all over Facebook!" She eyed Lanie's ring. "Sweetheart, I bet you made a beautiful bride."

Matt watched Marge rejoin her table and let out a deep breath. "Pictures?" he whispered to Lanie.

"Photoshop?"

"I'll see if I can arrange something." The colonel pulled out his phone to make a note.

Sadie reappeared from the kitchen with the check and dropped it on their table with a snort. Matt grabbed it and left two twenty-dollar bills inside the vinyl folder.

Showtime.

Whew! What will happen next?!
Click here to keep reading!

ALSO BY KERRY EVELYN

The Crane's Cove Series

Love on the Edge

A Night at the Inn: A Lizzie Borden Short Story

Love on the Rocks

Love on the Beach

Love on the Fly

The Cotton Candy Caper: A Fall Carnival Story (takes place within Love on the Beach's and Love on the Fly's time frames)

A Night in the Passage: A Crane's Cove Short Story (takes place within Love on the Fly's time frame)

The Fisherman Nutcracker: A Whimsical Christmas Story

A Night in the Cabin: A Crane's Cove Short Story

A Second Shot at Love

A Home for Christmas

ALSO BY KERRY EVELYN

The Cat's Paw Cove Series

Moon Mist Manor Book 1: Christmas at Moon Mist Manor

Moon Mist Manor Book 2: Love Overrules the Lawyer

Moon Mist Manor Book 3 The Beachcomber's Buccaneer Bounty

Letters from Eleanor: The Beginnings of Moon Mist Manor (newsletter serial; sign up at https://www.subscribepage.com/lettersfromeleanor)

Other Stories

Love on the Ice: A Hockey Romance Novelette

City Nights (How I Met My Other Anthology)

Fenway: A Beacon of Hope (How I Met My Other 2 Anthology)

Bird's Eye View (Once Upon Academy Anthology)

ACKNOWLEDGMENTS

Big thanks to the Big Guy upstairs who downloads stories into my head and heart, to my family for granting me the time to upload them to the page, and to the readers who love to get lost exploring my worlds!

Special thanks to my amazing writer friends for assisting in making these words shine their brightest—Angelique Bochnak, Megan Fuentes, Chelsea Fuchs, Stephanie Harrell, and Chris Kridler, and TJ Logan. Sarah's story may still be in my head if not for your love, time, and encouragement!

To the #Sweeties team—what a privilege, honor, and blessing it's been to work with you all! Your professionalism, generosity, love, and support has forever altered my perspective and changed me in the best of ways. I hope our paths cross again soon, and often!

ABOUT THE AUTHOR

Kerry Evelyn is the author of the Crane's Cove series, #sweet-resortromance with heart, healing, and happily-ever-afters set in Coastal Maine. She's also a Guest Author for the Cat's Paw Cove romance series and several short stories that span multiple genres. A native of the Massachusetts SouthCoast, Kerry changed her latitude in 2002 and now calls the Orlando area home. Fueled on faith, Dunkin' iced coffee, and a love for people, including her amazing family, Kerry loves (in ever-changing order) books, boybands, cats, hockey, sweet drinks, taking selfies, traveling, and the madness of getting the stories in her head onto the page.

Official Author Website:
https://kerryevelyn.com

Official Reader Facebook Group
www.facebook.com/groups/CranesCoveCrew

Facebook
@KerryEvelynAuthor

Instagram
@KerryEvelynAuthor

Twitter
@theKerryEvelyn

Amazon
www.amazon.com/Kerry-Evelyn/e/B077LWTYXJ

Goodreads Author Page
www.goodreads.com/author/show/17348375.Kerry_Evelyn

BookBub
www.bookbub.com/profile/kerry-evelyn

www.ingramcontent.com/pod-product-compliance
Lightning Source LLC
LaVergne TN
LVHW050944080826
845145LV00004B/1409

* 9 7 8 1 7 3 6 1 9 7 7 4 5 *